A NOTE TO PARENTS

One of the most important ways children learn to read — and learn to *like* reading — is by being with readers. Every time you read aloud, read along, or listen to your child read, you are providing the support that she or he needs as an emerging reader.

Disney's First Readers were created to make that reading time fun for you and your child. Each book in this series features characters that most children already recognize from popular Disney films. The familiarity and appeal of these high-interest characters will draw emerging readers easily into the story and at the same time support basic literacy skills, such as understanding that print has meaning, connecting oral language to written language, and developing cueing systems. And because Disney's First Readers are highly visual, children have another tool to help in understanding the text. This makes early reading a comfortable, confident experience — exactly what emerging readers need to become successful, fluent readers.

Read to Your Child

Here are a few hints to make early reading enjoyable and educational:

★ Talk with children before reading. Let them see how much they already know about the Disney characters. If they are unfamiliar with the movie basis of a book, take a few minutes to look at the cover and some of the illustrations to establish a context. Talking is important, since oral language precedes and supports reading.

★ Run your finger along the text to show that the words carry the story. Let your child read along if she or he recognizes that there are repeated words or phrases.

★ Encourage questions. A child's questions are good clues to his or her comprehension or thinking strategies.

★ Be prepared to read the same book several times. Children will develop ease with the story and concepts, so that later they can concentrate on reading and language.

Let Your Child Read to You

You are your child's best audience, so encourage her or him to read aloud to you often. And:

★ If children ask about an unknown word, give it to them. Don't interrupt the flow of reading to have them sound it out. However, if children start to sound out a word, let them.

★ Praise all reading efforts warmly and often!

—Patricia Koppman
Past President
International Reading Association

Paints and pencils by Sol Studios

Printed in the United States of America.

First Edition

1 3 5 7 9 10 8 6 4 2

Library of Congress Catalog Card Number: 97-80108

ISBN 0-7868-4170-2

Puppy Parade

by Cecilia Venn
Illustrated by Sol Studios

Disney's First Readers — Level 2
A Story from Disney's *101 Dalmatians*

Disney
PRESS

New York

Pongo said to Perdy,
"Where are our 99 pups?
We're very late for the Puppy Parade.
Wake up, my dear! Wake up!"

Perdy yawned and said to him,
"Don't worry, we'll find each one.
We'll look high and low for the puppies.
We won't stop until we are done."

First came Patch and Pepper.
They fell into a heap.
They woke up three puppies
who were fast asleep!

The five little puppies
rolled here and there.
They shook the lamp.
They bumped the chair.

Now five more puppies
were ready to go.
They rolled around
with a big pillow.
It landed on the floor,
in front of the T.V.
Lucky started barking.
He couldn't see!

Perdy looked around
and thumped her tail.
Five little puppies
spilled out of a pail.

One jumped into the laundry
to wipe off his nose.
He woke up Penny,
asleep in the clothes.

Five little puppies
started pulling a sock.
They pulled it so far
they banged into the clock.

The clock door flew open.
Five pups tumbled out.
Like a big spotted ball,
they rolled all about.

They rolled down the hallway
and out through the door.
Five fast puppies chased them.
Here come five more!

When the puppies reached
the kitchen,
they just could not stop.
They knocked over the basket,
the broom, and the mop.

The noise woke the puppies
who were napping in the sun.
They quickly jumped down
to join in the fun.

The last one to jump
knocked over a treat,
which Rolly and his pals
raced in to eat.

Five puppies peeked from
behind the door.
Five puppies hid inside a drawer.
Perdy looked everywhere
and kept finding more.

Perdy sniffed and
sniffed some more.
Then she heard something
scratching the floor.

She tiptoed over and
picked up the rug.
Five puppies ran out
and gave her a hug.

The other puppies rushed in.
The rug went flying.
It hit the piano bench,
where five more pups were lying.

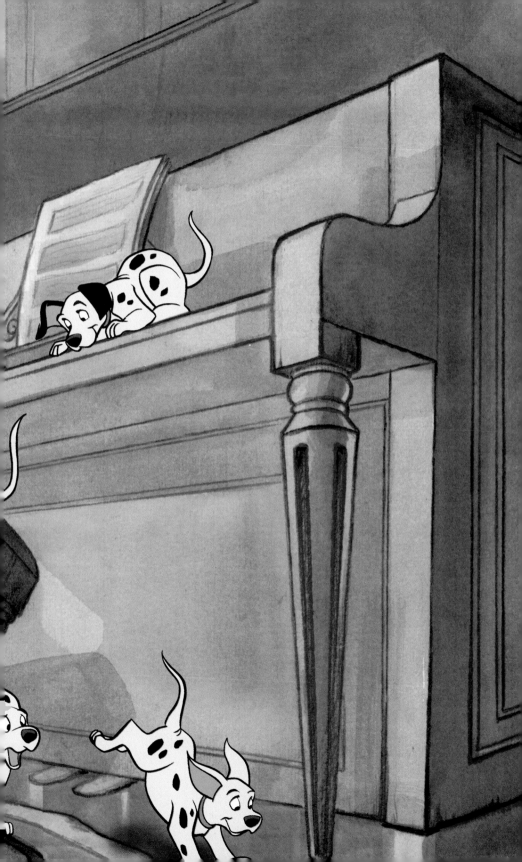

Those puppies popped up
and played a song.
Five more puppies joined them
and sang along.

Pongo counted each little head,
"5, 10, 15, 20, 25, 30, 35, 40, 45, 50,
55, 60, 65, 70, 75, 80, 85, 90
—only 95," he said.

Perdy scratched her head.
What could she do?
Then out came four puppies,
two pushing two.

Those last puppies got in line.
Pongo counted again.
"That's 99!"